W0009485

A GUINEA PIG

Romeo & Juliet

A GUINEA PIG

Romeo & Juliet

A pair of star-crossed lovers...

AN ADAPTATION OF THE ORIGINAL BY

Mr. WILLIAM
SHAKESPEARE

LONDON
BLOOMSBURY PUBLISHING, BEDFORD SQUARE.
2017

TROUPE OF ACTORS

MARLIN

BEAR

BILLIE

MABEL

OSCAR

SHERLOCK

MOLLY

DRAMATIS PERSONAE

ROMEO
of Montague

JULIET
of Capulet

MERCUTIO
Friend to Romeo

PRINCE OF VERONA
Keeper of the peace

TYBALT
Cousin to Juliet

FRIAR LAWRENCE
A monk

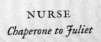

NURSE
Chaperone to Juliet

Three times have the great families of Capulet and Montague fought in the streets of Verona. To keep the peace, the Prince of Verona declares that if these mortal foes disturb the quiet again, they will pay with their lives.

Two households, both alike in dignity,
In fair Verona, where we lay our scene…

ACT I

Mercutio finds a lovesick Romeo walking in a grove of sycamore trees.

MERCUTIO: Good morning, Romeo.

ROMEO: Is the day so young? Ay me, sad hours seem long.

MERCUTIO: What sadness lengthens Romeo's hours?

ROMEO: In sadness, cousin, I love Rosaline,
yet she'll not be hit with Cupid's arrow.

ROMEO: *The all-seeing sun*
Never saw her match since first the world begun.

Mercutio invites Romeo to a banquet being held by the Capulets, hoping that Romeo will see other women more beautiful than Rosaline and be cured of his lovesickness.

MERCUTIO: At this same ancient feast of Capulet
Are all the admired beauties of Verona.
Compare Rosaline with some that I shall show,
And I will make thee think thy swan a crow.

Romeo and Mercutio set off for the Capulet banquet.

MERCUTIO: Come, gentle Romeo, the feast is done
And we shall come too late. We must have you dance.

ROMEO: *I fear too early, for my mind misgives*
Some consequence yet hanging in the stars...

Meanwhile in the Capulet household Juliet's Nurse gives her the surprising news that Paris, the local nobleman, wishes to marry her.

NURSE: Now you are almost fourteen, Juliet, tell me,
How stands your disposition to be married?

JULIET: It is an honour I dream not of.

NURSE: Well, think of marriage now:
The valiant Paris seeks you for his love
And does await you at the feast tonight.

Enter a servant to escort Juliet to the banquet.

NURSE: *Go, girl, seek happy nights to happy days.*

Romeo and Mercutio enter the banquet. Romeo forgets all about Rosaline when he sees Juliet.

ROMEO: What lady's that?
          O, she doth teach the torches to burn bright...

ROMEO: *Did my heart love till now? Forswear it, sight,*
For I ne'er saw true beauty till this night.

Romeo approaches Juliet to take her hand.

ROMEO: If I profane with my unworthiest hand
           This holy shrine, the gentle sin is this:
           My two lips, two blushing pilgrims, ready stand
           To smooth that rough touch with a tender kiss.

Juliet says it is no sin to hold hands.

JULIET: Good pilgrim, you do wrong your hand too much,
          Which mannerly devotion shows in this:
          For saints have hands that pilgrims' hands do touch,
          And palm to palm is holy palmers' kiss.

Juliet says that lips, like hands, should be used in prayer. Romeo asks if he might 'pray' to her...

ROMEO: Have not saints lips, and holy palmers too?

JULIET: Ay, pilgrim, lips that they must use in prayer.

ROMEO: O, then, dear saint, let lips do what hands do:
            They pray – grant thou, lest faith turn to despair.

JULIET: Saints do not move, though grant for prayers' sake.

Romeo leans forward to kiss her.

ROMEO: *Then move not, while my prayer's effect I take.*

The Nurse takes Juliet away, but Juliet keeps looking back at Romeo.

JULIET: What is yond gentleman, Nurse?

NURSE: His name is Romeo, and a Montague.
            The only son of your great enemy.

JULIET: *My only love sprung from my only hate!*
Too early seen unknown, and known too late!

❋ ACT II ❋

Romeo leaves the banquet when he discovers that Juliet is a Capulet, but then changes his mind.

ROMEO: Can I go forward when my heart is there?
          Turn back Romeo, and seek Juliet.

Romeo climbs over the wall and into the Capulet garden. He looks up and sees a light in a bedroom window.

ROMEO: *But soft! What light through yonder window breaks?*
           It is the east, and Juliet is the sun.

Juliet laments that Romeo is a Montague, but Romeo replies that he does not care about the rift between their families. They exchange vows of love and plan to marry the next day.

JULIET: O Romeo, Romeo! Wherefore art thou Romeo?
           What's in a name? That which we call a rose
           By any other name would smell as sweet.

ROMEO: It is my soul that calls upon my name.
           Call me but love, and I'll be new baptized.

JULIET: If that thy bent of love be honourable,
           Thy purpose marriage, send me word to-morrow.

JULIET: *Goodnight, goodnight! Parting is such sweet sorrow,*
That I shall say goodnight till it be morrow.

The next morning, Romeo asks Friar Lawrence to marry him to Juliet.

ROMEO: Holy father, my heart's dear love is set
On the fair daughter of rich Capulet.
I'll tell thee more anon, but this I pray,
That thou consent to marry us today.

Friar Lawrence agrees, sensing that this marriage could heal the grudge between the Montagues and Capulets.

FRIAR: For this alliance may so happy prove
To turn your households' rancour to pure Love.

Juliet impatiently waits in her bedroom while the Nurse talks to Romeo about plans for the wedding. When the Nurse returns, Juliet pesters her for news.

JULIET: Sweet, sweet, sweet Nurse, tell me, what says my love? What says Romeo?

NURSE: Have you got leave to go to church today?

JULIET: I have.

NURSE: Then hie you hence to Friar Lawrence's church.
There stays you a husband to make you a wife.

Romeo and Friar Lawrence wait for Juliet at the church.

ROMEO: Do thou but close our hands with holy words,
Then love-devouring death do what he dare,
It is enough I may but call her mine.

Enter Juliet, running late.

FRIAR: Here comes the lady.

FRIAR: *So smile the heavens upon this holy act...*

✵ ACT III ✵

Juliet's hot-headed cousin Tybalt challenges Romeo to a duel because he dared to come to the Capulet banquet, but Mercutio steps forward instead.

TYBALT: Romeo, thou art a villain. Turn and draw!

MERCUTIO: Come, sir, I am for you.

Tybalt and Mercutio fight. Tybalt thrusts his sword and strikes Mercutio.

MERCUTIO: I am hurt.
           A plague on both your houses!

He dies.

ROMEO: Now, Tybalt, Mercutio's soul
Is but a little way above our heads.
Either thou or I, or both, must go with him.

Romeo vanquishes Tybalt, then flees Verona as the Prince arrives
and declares Romeo's fate.

PRINCE: Who began this bloody fray?
          Romeo slew Tybalt, Tybalt slew Mercutio?
          Let Romeo hence in haste,
          Else, when he is found, that hour is his last.

PRINCE: *I will be deaf to pleading and excuses:*
Romeo is banishèd.

❋ ACT IV ❋

In despair at Romeo's banishment, Juliet visits Friar Lawrence to seek guidance; he gives her a sleeping potion that he says will help reunite her with Romeo.

FRIAR: Hold, daughter; I do spy a kind of hope.
Take thou this vial, being then in bed.
No warmth, no breath, shall testify thou livest;
Thou shalt be as dead two and forty hours,
And then awake as from a pleasant sleep.
That very night shall Romeo bear thee
Hence to Mantua.

JULIET: Romeo, Romeo, Romeo! I drink to thee.

In the morning, the Nurse comes in to wake Juliet but finds she cannot rouse her.

NURSE: Mistress! why, lady! fie, you slug-a-bed!
Why, love, I say! madam! sweet heart!
Marry and amen! How sound she is asleep!
I must needs wake you. Lady, lady, lady!

NURSE: *Alas, alas! Help, help! My lady's dead!*

ACT V

Mantua. Romeo meets a messenger bearing news of the death of Juliet.

ROMEO: News from Verona! How now, messenger?
Does thou not bring me letters from the Friar?
How fares my Juliet?

MESSENGER: Her body sleeps in Capulet's tomb,
And her immortal part with angels lives.

ROMEO: Is it so? Then I defy you, stars!

ROMEO: My Juliet, I will lie with thee tonight.
I will buy a dram of poison.

Romeo arrives at the Capulet tomb in Verona where Juliet lies.

ROMEO: Oh my love, my wife! Eyes, look your last,
                              Arms, take your last embrace; and lips...

He drinks the poison.

ROMEO: *Thus with a kiss I die.*

Juliet wakes from her drugged sleep and discovers Romeo lifeless beside her. She kisses him one last time, and decides that she would rather share his fate than live without him.

JULIET: Poison, I see, hath been his timeless end.
I kiss thy lips... thy lips are warm!

JULIET: *I'll be brief. O happy dagger,*
          I am thy sheath; there rest, and let me die.

The Prince arrives and summons the rival families of Romeo and Juliet
to show them the price of their feud.

PRINCE: A glooming peace this morning with it brings,
The sun, for sorrow, will not show his head.
For never was a story of more woe
Than this of Juliet and her Romeo.

The Montagues and Capulets pledge to live in peace and never forget their
beloved Romeo and Juliet.

Come, gentle night, and turn them into stars
And they will make the face of heaven so fine
That all the world will be in love with night.

WILLIAM SHAKESPEARE was born in Stratford-upon-Avon in 1564 and is widely regarded as the greatest writer in the English language. Also known as the Bard, he wrote more than thirty plays, including *Macbeth*, *Hamlet* and *A Midsummer Night's Dream*, which have been translated into every major living language and performed countless times over the past 450 years.

TESS NEWALL was born in 1987 and when she is not stitching tiny crowns or building miniature balconies she works as a freelance set designer, specializing in fashion, window displays and decorative interiors. She lives in London.

ALEX GOODWIN was born in 1985 and owns five different editions of *The Complete Works of William Shakespeare* (which he has been told is four too many). When he is not trimming soliloquies or pruning secondary characters, he works as an editor. He lives in London.

The publishers would like to thank Pauline, Rebecca, Amanda, Sophia and *ohmyguinea*'s Becky, as well as Charles, Ella, Edie, Barbara and our other friends for their kindness and for being such good company. Thanks also to the clever carpenter, Alfred. A particular thank you to photographer and designer Phillip Beresford, without whom the torches of guinea pig Verona would burn less brightly.

Small pets are abandoned every day, but the lucky ones end up in rescue centres where they can be looked after and rehomed. You may not know it, but some of these centres are devoted entirely to guinea pigs. They work with welfare organizations to give first class advice and information, as well as finding happy new homes for the animals they look after. If you, like Romeo and Juliet, dream of a more loving world, perhaps think of supporting your local rescue centre!

Bloomsbury Publishing
An imprint of Bloomsbury Publishing Plc

50 Bedford Square
London
WC1B 3DP
UK

1385 Broadway
New York
NY 10018
USA

www.bloomsbury.com

BLOOMSBURY and the Diana logo are trademarks of Bloomsbury Publishing Plc

First published in Great Britain 2017

Abridgement and photography © Bloomsbury Publishing Plc, 2017

Alex Goodwin and Phillip Beresford have asserted their right under the Copyright, Designs and Patents Act, 1988,
to be identified as Author and Photographer respectively of this work.

British Library Cataloguing-in-Publication Data
A catalogue record for this book is available from the British Library.

Library of Congress Cataloguing-in-Publication data has been applied for.

ISBN UK: HB: 978-1-4088-9064-6
ISBN US: HB: 978-1-63557-000-7

2 4 6 8 10 9 7 5 3

Costumes and props by Tess Newall
Photography and design by Phillip Beresford
Abridgement by Alex Goodwin
Illustration on page 2 by Elizabeth Stettler

Printed and bound in China by C&C Offset Printing Co., Ltd

All papers used by Bloomsbury Publishing Plc are natural, recyclable products made from wood grown in well-managed forests.
Our manufacturing processes conform to the environmental regulations of the country of origin.